TOP 10 TIPS FOR BUILDING FRIENDSHIPS

DALE-MARIE BRYAN

ROSEN
PUBLISHING®

NEW YORK

Published in 2013 by The Rosen Publishing Group, Inc.
29 East 21st Street, New York, NY 10010

Library of Congress Cataloging-in-Publication Data

Bryan, Dale-Marie, 1953–
Top 10 tips for building friendships/Dale-Marie Bryan. — 1st ed.
     p. cm. — (Tips for success)
Includes bibliographical references and index.
ISBN 978-1-4488-6859-9 (library binding)
1. Friendship. 2. Self-presentation. I. Title. II. Title: Top ten tips for building friendships.
BF575.F66.B793 2013
158.2'5—dc23
                                                          2012001100

Manufactured in the United States of America

CPSIA Compliance Information: Batch #S12YA: For further information, contact Rosen Publishing, New York, New York, at 1-800-237-9932.

CONTENTS

INTRODUCTION 4

TIP #1 BECOME A FRIENDSHIP DETECTIVE 7

TIP #2 BE YOUR OWN BEST FRIEND 12

TIP #3 LEARN THE UNWRITTEN RULES 16

TIP #4 KEEP IT REAL: SHOW THE TRUE YOU 21

TIP #5 LISTEN UP: LEARN TO LISTEN 25

TIP #6 WATCH WHAT YOU SAY 30

TIP #7 LEARN TO GIVE AND TAKE 34

TIP #8 BRANCH OUT: EXPAND YOUR FRIENDSHIP POSSIBILITIES 38

TIP #9 BE A SAFE AND SAVVY CYBER FRIEND 42

TIP #10 WEATHER THE BUMPS 47

GLOSSARY 52
FOR MORE INFORMATION 53
FOR FURTHER READING 56
BIBLIOGRAPHY 58
INDEX 62

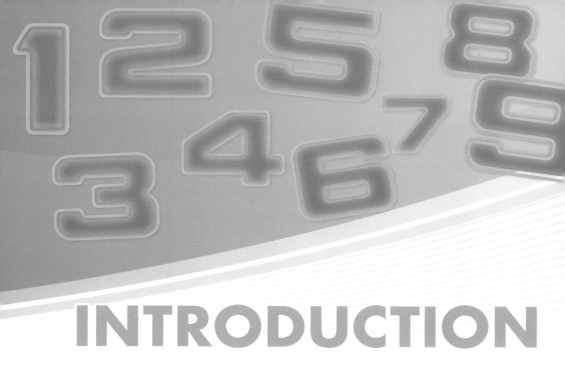

INTRODUCTION

uds. BFFs. Friends. Most people want them. Everyone needs them. But what makes a person a friend? Why are friends important? And how do we make friends in the first place? If you've asked yourself any of these questions, you aren't alone. Friendship has probably been a topic for discussion since humans began rubbing elbows around their cave campfires.

In Merriam-Webster's online dictionary, a friend is defined as "one attached to another by affection or esteem." Maybe you thought being friends was people simply liking each other. It's the "attached" part that makes a friendship more. Being friends with another person means you share a bond built on common interests or goals. You may be in the same classes at school or belong to the same religious congregation. Maybe you are both the middle children in your families. On the other hand, you can

Good ways to keep friendships healthy are to spend time relaxing together and appreciating each other's talents.

be drawn to friends because you are different, too. It's those differences that make you interesting and exciting to each other. But whatever draws you together doesn't really matter. It's the affection and respect friends have for each other that glue the relationship together.

Friends are the people we choose to spend time with in good times and bad. They are the first people we text, call, or e-mail with exciting news. They are also the ones we lean on and talk to when things aren't going so well. Whether making friends is easy for you or seems harder than climbing Mt. Everest, it's important to become better at a skill that affects you now and can help you in future relationships.

What are the benefits of friendship? Well, for one, having a friend means you always have someone to go places and do things with. You don't have to be alone unless you want to be.

Having friends is also healthy for you. Studies cited in a *New York Times* article by Tara Parker-Pope showed that people with friends tend to live longer and are better able to fight illnesses. People with friends are less likely to be depressed, too. Plus, friends support us and challenge us to be our best. A 2007 study at the University of Virginia showed that people who faced the challenge of climbing a steep hill carrying a heavy backpack did not think the hill was as steep when they were with friends.

The types of friendships you have when you are young affect your future, according to a study at the University of Oregon Child and Family Center. The study followed middle school students and found that young people that had friends who worked for good grades were more successful in college and after graduation.

This book presents ten ways to build these types of positive friendships. You will learn about different kinds of friendships and how being friends with yourself is an important first step. You will also learn the characteristics of a good friend and ways you can be a good friend to others. Discovering what kind of friend you are and what to expect from a friendship can help you improve your friendship-building skills. These skills will help you succeed in future relationships.

BECOME A FRIENDSHIP DETECTIVE

For some people, making friends is easy. There's the laughing guy in the middle of the lunchroom group and the smiling girl who people always crowd around in the hall. Why are they so lucky? What makes them so special? What do they have?

The answer is: nothing that you don't have. Just because a person attracts people like ants to sugar doesn't mean all of those people are close friends. It is likely his or her popularity has little to do with the true nature of friendship.

Some people are born with the knack to attract people. Others just naturally know the tricks of the friend-making trade. The funny thing is, they probably couldn't tell you what those

There are different types of friends, from people you laugh with at lunchtime to confidants whom you'll tell your deepest secrets. It's natural to be closer to some friends than others.

tricks are. But you can become a detective and learn by observing those "lucky" ones yourself.

DIFFERENT KINDS OF FRIENDS

First, it's important to understand that there are different levels of friendship. Aristotle, the great thinker and scientist of ancient Greece, said there are three types of friends: those who are useful, those who are pleasant, and those who are good. What did he mean? Useful friends are what we think of as casual friends, or acquaintances, today. Casual friends may say "hi" in the hall or exchange homework notes for class. They may even sit together in the cafeteria. But the reason they are friends is that they are useful

QUALITIES OF A GOOD FRIEND

If you could give friendships grades, what kind of friend would get an A+? Here are some characteristics to look for in a good friend. A healthy friend is:

- fair
- honest
- respectful
- caring
- fun to be with
- a good listener
- willing to help you
- someone who brings out your best
- there for you in good times and bad
- a person who likes you for who you are

A good friend is like a favorite sweater. She is a good fit and warms you when times are cold.

to each other in some way. They fill a need for each other (such as help with schoolwork or company at lunchtime). They don't have deep feelings for each other or seek each other out in times of trouble or happiness. Relationships with useful friends are brief.

Pleasant friends are people you like to do things with. They are great to be around, and you like each other's company. But they aren't necessarily the friends you can count on when times are tough. As you can guess, this type of friendship doesn't last a long time either.

Good friends are those that have long-term relationships. Good friends both respect and care about each other and accept the other person as he or she is. Of Aristotle's three, this is the type

SIGNS OF AN UNHEALTHY FRIENDSHIP

It's also important to be able to identify unhealthy friendships. This knowledge can help you to avoid these kinds of poisonous relationships. An unhealthy friend:

- is negative
- is full of put-downs
- makes you feel like you can't be yourself
- encourages behaviors that go against your beliefs
- always pressures you to give in
- excludes others
- makes you feel uneasy, uncomfortable, ashamed, or guilty
- distracts you from your goals and dreams
- doesn't encourage your growth or make you a better person

of friend that could be called a true friend. It takes time for these kinds of friendships to develop. "Wishing to be friends," he said, "is quick work, but friendship is a slow-ripening fruit."

THE CHANGING FACE OF FRIENDSHIP

The types of friends we have often changes as we grow up. Around two years old, children begin to relate to others their own age. From then until about age four, they are friends with the person they are playing with at the moment. In kindergarten and first grade, children start to realize that other people have different ideas and personalities.

At ages seven, eight, and nine, a child's friendship circle grows. Children start to relate based on what they like and dislike about individuals. Friendship is also related to what each person needs from the other. At this age, children are better at cooperating and sharing. They are more aware of others' feelings.

In late elementary and middle school, young people build relationships around activities. They begin to feel the pressure of fitting in. Cliques form, and there may be rules for being accepted into them. As they get older, teens start to spend more time with their friends than they do with their families, and they are more likely to share their feelings.

It's easier to understand friend relationships when you can observe those of others and compare them. Knowing that relationships change with age helps explain why friendship can become more challenging.

BE YOUR OWN BEST FRIEND

You are the one person you can count on spending the rest of your life with. So it's important to become your own best friend. That can be hard in your teens because it's a time when you are figuring out exactly who you are. But there are good reasons to try.

People who don't feel good about themselves aren't very good company. And nothing pushes others away more than anger or gloom and doom. Shyness can also be a barrier to reaching out. But remember, everyone feels shy and insecure in certain situations. The more you learn about yourself, the more confidence you'll have.

Be careful about putting yourself down. Some people get into that habit because they lack confidence: they believe they are saying only what others think. But when you respect and believe in yourself, others will believe in you, too.

WAYS TO BE GOOD TO YOURSELF

Treating yourself well is part of being your own best friend. Here are some ways to do that:

- Give yourself a break. You can't be on top of your game all the time. If you goof up, do what you can to make it right. Then move on.
- Eating healthy foods, exercising, and getting plenty of sleep really do make you feel better.
- If you have an attack of shyness in a new situation, think about your many positive qualities. Stand up straight and put your shoulders back. Remember that everyone in the room has bed head or morning breath at times.
- Find something to laugh about every day. Laughter relieves stress and increases your self-esteem.
- Do something you enjoy every day.

FIXING YOUR MENTAL MIRROR

Being your own best friend is all about improving your self-esteem. Self-esteem is how you see yourself in your mental mirror. Your past experiences and exchanges with other people have implanted an image in your brain. This image affects how you accept and value yourself. If it's not a picture you like to see, you have the tools and talent to change it.

How can you improve your self-image and become your own best friend? A good beginning is to envision a giant eraser.

Imagine using the eraser on the part of your brain that thinks up hurtful things about you. Every time you have a negative thought about yourself, erase it and replace it with a positive one. For example, you might think, "I run slower than syrup drips." Stop, erase, and replace that thought with: "I may be a slow runner, but I'm a walking dictionary!"

MAKE A "ME" LIST

Next, try dividing a piece of paper into four sections, all about you. Label one "What I Like" and another "What I Don't Like." Label the third and fourth sections "What I'm Good At" and "Ways I'd Like to Improve." Then think about and write down characteristics and actions you like and dislike about yourself. Write down your strongest skills and target areas you'd like to improve. Keep the list handy and add to it when you think of new ideas. Writing these

Be proud of the things you can do well. Be ready to learn new skills.

things down will help you organize your thoughts and allow you to recognize who you really are.

Setting reasonable goals and trying new things is important. Reaching goals gives you a boost and improves your confidence. Also, when you learn to do something new, it not only makes you feel good, but it can also open up opportunities to meet new people and make more friends.

Accepting yourself as you are is part of being your best friend, too. You are unique and special. There is no one else like you in the world. When you try to be like others, it's like trying to put on a too-tight shirt. It will never feel right no matter how much you pull and stretch it. So put that shirt away! It's your uniqueness that makes you interesting to others. Be proud to be different.

LEARN THE UNWRITTEN RULES

Now that you know a little about the different types of friendships and are getting a handle on your mental mirror, it's time to think about communication skills. How well do you communicate with others? Are you giving people the messages you mean to?

COMMUNICATION PLUS

There are many ways to communicate besides talking. Your body language, clothing choices, gestures, facial expressions, choice of where to stand (such as too close or too far away), and touching or not touching are all ways you "speak" without words. Another way to communicate is with paralanguage. Paralanguage refers to the special characteristics of your voice,

NONVERBAL WAYS TO COMMUNICATE FRIENDLINESS

Have you ever encountered an angry dog? He can't talk, but you can tell he is angry by the snarling teeth, prickled fur, and piercing glare. You communicate your feelings without talking, too. Here are some ways to show you are open and welcoming, and want to be friends:

- If you get nervous in new situations, try to relax your body and smile. If you feel tense, take deep breaths and picture yourself in a place where you feel comfortable and relaxed, such as in a warm bath or on a beach.
- Be aware of how you respond to others when they are talking. Show interest by nodding your head and smiling.
- Make eye contact to let the speaker know he or she has your full attention.
- Respect the other person's "body bubble." Imagine the person standing in a hula hoop, and avoid getting any closer.
- Watch the tone of your voice and facial expressions. Make sure to match them to the words you use.

An old saying goes, "The eyes are the windows to the soul." Keeping your "windows" open to others lets them know you care.

such as how loudly or softly you speak and what speed and tone you use. It also includes the noises people make, such as humming or whistling.

Making eye contact is also important in communication. Looking people in the eye shows confidence. It also tells others you can be trusted.

ACTIONS ARE WORTH A THOUSAND WORDS

Have you ever rolled your eyes when someone said something you didn't want to hear? Or maybe you have slid down in your

WHAT TO DO IF YOU'RE SHY

Communicating with confidence can be challenging if you are shy . Here are some strategies to try:

- Say "hi" when people greet you. Not answering or looking away could give them the impression that you are stuck-up.
- If you know a person's name, say it when you greet him or her.
- Encourage yourself. Replace negative thoughts about yourself with positive ones. Change "I can't do this" to "Yes, I can!"
- Picture yourself as confident in social situations.
- Don't beat yourself up if you make a mistake. Remember that others don't notice your mistakes as much as you do.
- Don't always wait to be invited. Join the group. Standing at the edge keeps you there.
- Give honest compliments. Everyone appreciates them.

desk when your teacher was asking for volunteers. You are sending messages with these actions without opening your mouth.

You receive messages from others, too. How does it make you feel if someone you don't know stands too close? Do you want to cover your ears if someone talks in a loud, nasally voice? These reactions are your response to the messages you are receiving.

The wordless messages we send and receive can affect the way people view us. In fact, some people say our behaviors give more information than the words we use. And just as there are grammar rules for what we say and write, there are unwritten rules for how we act and react.

Standing close to a good friend is one thing. Standing close to someone you don't know well can seem threatening.

MIXED MESSAGES

We learn many of these rules of relating to others naturally as children. They become second nature to us as we interact with other people. But some people don't understand. Something disrupts their learning, and the messages we send to them pass them by. They may not know their actions are sending messages, too, and they feel hurt and confused when they can't connect. As you can imagine, not knowing the unwritten social rules can affect a person's success at forming relationships. So what can you do if you don't know all the rules? Is it possible to change the messages you send?

You can become more skilled at sending and receiving messages. One way is to become conscious of, and to carefully observe, how people act in social situations. Go to the mall or to a sporting event—any place where people interact. Do some people watching. What do you notice about how people react to each other? Can you tell the friends from the strangers? What can you tell from their body language? Listen to people talk. Notice the volume and tone of their voices.

Now think about how people react to you. Are you the person who stands with your head high? Do you smile if someone catches your eye? Or are you the one who casts your eyes down and moves away if people get near? Everyone has different comfort levels when it comes to communicating, but becoming aware of the silent code of communication can help you as you navigate your social sea.

KEEP IT REAL: SHOW THE TRUE YOU

The most important element you can bring to a friendship is your true self. Too often we think we have to change into something we're not to make people like us. Reality TV shows make it appear that way. But you don't need a makeover to make friends. Real friends accept each other as they are.

Of course, it can be scary to let the "real" you show. We all hold up our defense shields to keep ourselves from getting hurt. But putting up barriers keeps us from great relationships. So be brave. Lower the armor a little, and be real!

One of the most important ways to be real is to be honest. Friends depend on us to tell them what we really think. Of course, you don't need to say "Terrible!" when a friend asks you how her new jeans look. But you could say something like, "Those are

Each person in a friendship should be equally important. Real friends strive for a balance of power and don't try to dominate each other.

nice, but I've always liked your other ones, too." Weigh your words before you speak, and be sure to mix your honesty with kindness.

IN FRIENDS WE TRUST

Being honest also means keeping your word. If you make plans together, follow through and show up on time. If your friend asks you to go to the mall and you don't want to, be honest and say so. Don't make up a lame excuse not to go. Sure, your friend may never find out, but if you lie and are caught, he or she may never completely trust you again.

Another way to be real is to stand up for yourself. You don't have to agree on everything to stay friends with someone. Part of the fun of having friends is learning new ways of thinking and having different experiences. However, that doesn't mean you have to give in on everything. You have the right to your own opinions. You should also have the freedom to say no. If you

WAYS TO DEVELOP TRUST

Trust doesn't happen overnight. People prove themselves trustworthy through their deeds over time. Here are some ways to develop trustworthiness in a relationship:

- Be on time. Call or text if you are going to be late.
- Keep your word. If you say you're going to be somewhere, be there.
- Tell the truth, but kindly. Weigh your words to test their hurtfulness. Be honest but not brutal.
- Keep secrets safe. However, if a friend tells you a secret involving a person being hurt, you must get help from a trusted adult. You aren't being a bad friend by telling. You are helping protect the person from further harm.
- Offer to help, and follow through, when your friend is having a tough time.
- Be courageous. Do the right thing, including standing up for others.

really don't want to try sushi, you don't have to. You can make your own choices.

BEING YOUR BEST

A good friend will inspire you to be your best self. Sure, you still may get nervous and talk too loud once in a while. You may do dumb things you wish you hadn't. For the most part, though, a true friend will bring out your good side, and the not-so-good things about you will take a back seat.

Being real also means you must accept imperfection. Things won't always go smoothly. Even the best friendships have their ups and downs. Be realistic about what you expect from your friendship. Just because you are friends doesn't mean you have to spend every minute together. It's healthy for you and your friend to have a life beyond each other. And if your friend wants to make plans with others sometimes, that's no reflection on you.

You need to be realistic about your friend, too. Since nobody is perfect, be prepared to have hurt feelings at times. She may not compliment your new haircut. Or he might let it slip that you're afraid of clowns. Wait until you're alone and tell your friend how you feel. Then let it go. Most of the time, friends don't mean to be hurtful. They are just being human.

LISTEN UP: LEARN TO LISTEN

Being a good listener is more than just taking out your ear buds when someone is talking. There is nothing more irritating than telling a friend about the cute guy or girl in your algebra class, only to have the friend say, "Huh?" when you're halfway through. Listening is more than just hearing sounds. Learning to listen takes practice. It also takes maturity and a willingness to listen actively.

Learning to listen well when you are young will make life easier for you in school and at home by helping you avoid conflict with teachers and parents. It will also help you become a better friend because people feel cared about and respected when others value what they say.

An active listener must be observant. What do the speaker's body language and expressions tell you about what the person is saying?

HEARING THE THOUGHTS BEHIND THE WORDS

Active listening is focusing on what a person says in order to understand and ask questions about it. It involves listening to receive the message and deciding what it means. The key to active listening is to concentrate on the thoughts and feelings behind the speaker's words. It also involves keeping an open mind so you can understand the person's point of view and relate to it without judging.

BE AN ACTIVE LISTENER

The following are five ways to be all ears in a conversation:

- Listen with your ears, heart, and mind.
- Turn off your cell phone.
- Show you are listening with direct eye contact, facial expressions, and encouraging comments.
- Be careful about giving advice. Sometimes when people tell us their problems, we think they expect us to solve them. But mostly they just want someone to listen.
- Show compassion.

Often, we don't listen well because we are too busy thinking of what we want to say next. Then we don't focus on the other person's message. We're just waiting for the person to stop talking so we can jump in. That can lead to confusion on both sides.

Another obstacle to listening well is the fact that we have so much clamoring for our attention. This can make it hard to concentrate and listen. Admit it: how many times have you been tempted to check your text messages or answer your cell phone when a friend is talking? Think, too, about how it feels when someone chooses their technology over your latest train of thought. We have to make a real effort to listen, and that can be hard to do in our overstimulated world.

We are also conditioned not to listen. How many commercials do you really hear after the first time? And do you really hear your mother when she tells you to be careful when you go out the door?

LISTENING WELL TAKES PRACTICE

It's not hard to learn to listen. But it takes work to become good at it. First, put away or turn off all technology. Next, face the person you are about to listen to. Meet your friend's eyes and clear your mind of everything but what he or she is saying. Think about the person's feelings. Is he or she angry, worried, or stressed? Try to keep your own feelings and opinions out of the conversation. Show that you have understood what your friend has said by stating the main points in your own words. If you don't understand something the person said, ask questions to clarify. Begin your response by saying something like: "It sounds like you are really worried about…"

Your body language is also part of listening. Crossing your arms can create the impression of a wall between you and what your friend has to say. If you look away or at your watch, he or she may think you are bored or don't have time to listen. You can show you are listening through your expressions and how you respond. Saying "Uh, huh," or "Really?" at the right times lets the person know you are mentally "there." So do nodding, frowning, and smiling. An old saying sums up a good rule: Since we have two ears and one mouth, we should listen twice as much as we talk.

MYTHS & FACTS

MYTH: FRIENDSHIPS HAVE NO EFFECT ON YOUR HEALTH.

FACT: RESEARCH HAS SHOWN THAT HAVING FRIENDS CAN MAKE YOU HAPPIER AND HEALTHIER. ACCORDING TO THE UNIVERSITY OF CAMBRIDGE AND THE MRC NATIONAL SURVEY FOR HEALTH AND DEVELOPMENT, HAVING AT LEAST ONE FRIEND KEEPS TEENS FROM WITHDRAWING AND BEING DEPRESSED. AS PEOPLE AGE, HAVING STRONG SOCIAL TIES IS ASSOCIATED WITH LOWER BLOOD PRESSURE AND LONGER LIFE EXPECTANCIES, ACCORDING TO HARVARD MEDICAL SCHOOL.

MYTH: EVERYONE NEEDS A BEST FRIEND.

FACT: NOT EVERYONE NEEDS A BEST FRIEND, AND SOMETIMES HAVING A BEST FRIEND CAN BE VERY RESTRICTIVE. HAVING A FEW GOOD AND CLOSE FRIENDS IS OFTEN MORE IMPORTANT.

MYTH: IT'S IMPOSSIBLE FOR GUYS AND GIRLS TO BE FRIENDS.

FACT: FRIENDSHIP WITH SOMEONE OF THE OPPOSITE SEX IS DEFINITELY POSSIBLE. IT CAN BE A LOT OF FUN, AND IT GIVES YOU A CHANCE TO GLIMPSE LIFE FROM ANOTHER POINT OF VIEW. DON'T BE SURPRISED, THOUGH, IF OTHER KIDS TEASE THAT YOU ARE MORE THAN FRIENDS.

TIP #6

WATCH WHAT YOU SAY

We learn to talk when we are little. So we should know how to do it by now, right? If only that were the case! As you've probably found out, talking with someone you are meeting for the first time is not always easy. It's hard to talk to friends sometimes, too, especially if the topic is something you disagree about. For many people, holding conversations is challenging. Some think it's because we are communicating more through technology and are forgetting how to talk face-to-face. How many people do you know that would rather send a text than talk to someone in person? It does take work learning to carry on meaningful conversations. But it can be done with practice and by learning some conversational basics.

Conversation is an art. Just as in painting or drawing, it takes practice to learn to do it well.

REMEMBER THE LISTENING RULES

Many of the same tips for being an active listener apply to having a good conversation. For example, making eye contact keeps your friend's attention. In addition, your body language, expressions, and gestures often tell your listener as much as your words do.

Be aware of your tone of voice and volume. Your message can change if you sound sarcastic or angry. Someone who speaks too softly is difficult to listen to. The same goes for a person who is too loud.

Besides the way you speak, you need to think about what you say. It's easy to alter your words before they come out of your

BE A CREATIVE CONVERSATIONALIST

Sometimes it's hard to think of things to talk about when you want to start a conversation, especially with someone new. Remember that people like it when you show interest in them. Here are some questions to ask to get people talking about themselves:

- I wish the cafeteria served pizza more often. What about you?
- I can't wait for spring break. Are you doing anything special?
- Aren't you in my math class? What did you think of that quiz?
- I like basketball. What's your favorite sport?
- My little brother is a pain. Do you have any brothers or sisters?
- I've got a cat. Do you have any pets?

mouth but impossible afterward. So before you speak, consider how what you are about to say will affect the other person.

If you are meeting someone for the first time, discuss something you have in common, such as school or sports. Also remember that most people like to talk about themselves. Note something about the person and ask a question or make a comment, such as, "Wow! I can't believe you can eat those jalapeños. They make my nose burn!" It helps to give sincere compliments, too. "I love that shade of blue in your shirt. It looks good on you."

USE "I" MESSAGES

When you are having a difficult conversation with a friend, it can be helpful to use "I" messages instead of "You" messages. An I message is a statement in which you tell your feelings about something. For example, instead of saying "You make me so mad when you ignore me!" your statement would be, "I feel left out when I don't hear from you." I messages help people express their feelings without insulting or blaming others. And it puts the feelings in the right place. Your friend isn't responsible for your feelings. You are. But your friend won't know how you feel unless you tell him or her. Using I messages allows you to express your feelings without trampling on someone else's.

LOCK THE LIPS, EXCEPT WHEN...

Watch what you say about other people online and offline. Gossiping, or spreading rumors, is not a good idea: it can hurt others, and it has a way of coming back to haunt you.

You also need to be careful about other things you might say. You and your friends may share information about yourselves or your families. But that information is for your ears only, not for the masses. If you're not sure a friend would want you to repeat something, don't say or write it, even if your friend hasn't told you to keep the information secret.

Keeping secrets when you are told something in confidence is important to a friendship. Even if your relationship ends, that's not a green light to share your friend's secrets. Think about how you would feel if he or she did that to you.

At the same time, it's important to know which secrets not to keep in a friendship. If a secret involves abuse of any kind or someone getting hurt in another way, you must tell. Your friend needs the kind of help you can't provide. You must tell a trusted adult to get the kind of help your friend needs.

TIP #7

LEARN TO GIVE AND TAKE

We all bring our strengths and weaknesses, likes and dislikes, and similarities and differences to relationships. These qualities, along with the experiences we have, shape us into the people we are and provide the reasons friends connect with us in the first place. They also determine what we have to give in relationships and what we need to take from others.

Part of reaching out to others and making friends is recognizing our needs and what we have to share. Remember the "Me" list you began earlier in this book? Refer to it now as you think about what you have to offer.

FILLING IN THE GAPS

Maybe you're a math whiz, but you stink at writing essays. Your friend may have a strong family unit, but yours has been feeling rocky. No one is good at everything or has the perfect life. We

WAYS TO SAY NO AND STAY COOL

It's possible to outsmart peer pressure if you are prepared. Memorize a few good "excuses" that will allow you to exit an uncomfortable situation gracefully. Come up with statements that you feel comfortable saying and that fit your personality. You can also develop strategies to help you avoid participating in risky activities. Here are a few examples:

- Use your parents as an excuse. "No, thanks. My parents would kill me if I..."
- Use evidence. "No way! I saw pictures of smokers' lungs, and it made me sick."
- Keep a glass of water or soda in your hand at a party. If someone offers, you already have a drink.
- Keep your cell phone handy and plan an exit strategy with your parents. If you call to say you've got an upset stomach or a splitting headache, they'll know it's code to come pick you up.
- Don't be afraid to ask a trusted adult for help if a situation seems unsafe.
- Follow your instincts. If it doesn't seem right, don't do it.

can't help these influences or who we are. But friends help us fill the gaps. We grow when we help others, and others grow when we allow them to help us.

Remember that friends don't keep score. The give-and-take in friendships is seldom perfectly balanced, and that's normal. Your friend might need a lot of your time this year while he or she works through a tough situation. But it's likely you'll be leaning on him or her soon enough with your own problems.

One of most rewarding things about friendship is having someone to pursue and enjoy your interests with. But even that involves give-and-take. Sometimes you'll participate in activities you both love. Other times you'll want to do your favorite thing. Being willing to go along with each other's ideas presents opportunities to learn from each other and to master new skills.

PEERS, NOT PARENTS

When you are in your teens, you are working on figuring out who you are. You may find yourself looking more to your peers than your parents as models. Most of the time, this is healthy as you observe others your age and test out and share new ideas. Peer

Saying no is an act of courage. It might not win you any medals, but you'll be able to respect yourself afterward.

influence can be positive, especially if you and your friends have similar values. For example, if you hang out with friends who get good grades, it's likely you will, too, because you will work to fit in with your group.

The influence people your age have on you is called peer pressure. As you can see, it's not always bad, especially when peers influence each other to do the right thing. The downside of peer pressure is that some young people are tempted to take part in behaviors that go against their beliefs. Drugs, drinking, or smoking may come to mind first. Peers can also pressure you to bully, shoplift, go against authorities or parents, or have sex before you're ready.

If you are being pressured to do things that are risky or that make you uncomfortable, you are likely involved in the unhealthy form of friendship. You might consider caving in to these pressures because you want to fit in or are worried about being teased. However, if one person can have the courage to say no, it makes it easier for others to stand up against peer pressure. Standing up for your beliefs is hard, but you'll gain respect from others. You'll have more respect for yourself, too.

BRANCH OUT:
EXPAND YOUR
FRIENDSHIP POSSIBILITIES

A new boy moved into the neighborhood, and he shoots baskets by himself after school. You're pretty good at baskets, too, and he looks like he could use a friend. The only problem is, he's a guy and you're a girl.

Guy and girl friendships can be awesome but tricky! One reason is that male and female brains operate differently. According to author and counselor Michael Gurian, boys and girls relate, experience emotions, and pay attention in different ways. Because of these variations, boys tend to be more action-oriented, and girls tend to understand emotions and words better. These differences can lead to misunderstandings. But having friends of the opposite sex means more opportunities to see and understand how "the other side" manages in the world.

A girl you know is gay. She's smart and funny and you have a lot in common. Is it possible to be friends even though you're

STAY TRUE TO YOU

Knowing who you are and embracing your uniqueness can be powerful. Here are some ways to do that:

- **Stand up for yourself. If you don't like something, say so and give reasons.**
- **Work on your self-esteem. Replace negative thoughts about yourself with positive pats on the back.**
- **Look for ways to be the real you. If you like your hair short and spiky, wear it that way.**
- **Take people who tease or make negative comments by surprise. Reply with a humorous or positive thought.**
- **Be proud to be different. Encourage others to be proud of their differences, too.**

straight? People of a different sexual orientation can be wonderful friends. Friendship is about loyalty, honesty, and enjoying each other's company, not whether a person is gay or straight, a guy or a girl.

Don't be surprised, however, if others tease you about being friends with someone of the opposite sex or a different sexual orientation. Sadly, it's one of the drawbacks of being willing to branch out and try something different. Like animals, humans notice others of their kind who act differently and not always in a good way. The important thing to remember is that the quality of your friendship is what matters, not what others say about it. So stick up for each other and your right to be friends. Try to ignore the hurtful things that less-informed people might say. Usually, if a teaser doesn't get a reaction from you, he or she will give up and move on. Even better, think of ways you can turn the situation positive, such as inviting the teaser to join you in an activity.

ALL IN THE FAMILY

Sometimes we have built-in friends in our families. According to Stephen Bank and Michael Kahn, psychologists and authors of *The Sibling Bond*, relationships between brothers and sisters affect us more and last longer than other kinds of relationships, even those with our parents! The way a child gets along with a brother or sister can affect how he or she gets along with others. Even if they argue at times, siblings tend to learn how to cooperate and be friendlier to others. According to research by psychologist Brian Bigelow, experiencing moderate conflict makes brothers and sisters better equipped to deal with relationships outside the family.

Brothers and sisters (or other family members, such as cousins) can be built-in friends.

FRIENDS IN BULK

It is possible to have a best friend, but contrary to what you may think, not everyone does. Having a group of friends can be fun, too. According to data from the Pew Internet & American Life Project, because of technology, today's teens have larger groups of friends that they keep in touch with regularly than they did in the past.

Being part of a group means you'll have a supportive team behind you when you perform your speech or try out for the school play. The kinship you feel as part of a unit also increases a person's self-esteem.

Being part of a group of friends does have challenges, though. Instead of being mindful of a single person's ideas, schedule, and feelings, you have to consider those of multiple people. Also, doing most activities with a large group may limit the time you have to relate to others one-on-one.

BE OPEN TO NEW PEOPLE AND IDEAS

Remaining your own person within a group can be difficult, too. Sometimes it may seem easier to go along with the group than to follow your own desires. Also, groups of friends can become exclusive. These kinds of groups are known as cliques. The members of a clique may begin to follow someone else's rules instead of their own. The rules could be about who is accepted or what members can wear. At times, a clique can encourage hurtful behavior that individuals might not have thought of or wanted to do on their own.

A great way to branch out and meet others is to look for new activities to be involved in. Whether scuba diving or scouts, in school or out, there are many groups that band together to pursue their interests. They also enjoy teaching others to appreciate the same hobbies.

BE A SAFE AND SAVVY CYBER FRIEND

It's no surprise that technology is affecting the way friends relate these days. According to a report from the Nielsen Company, American teens sent an average of 3,364 texts a month in the first quarter of 2011. That's a lot of keystrokes. And eleven- to fourteen-year-olds leave their parents in the dust when it comes to media multitasking. They spend a total of nearly twelve hours a day watching television, using the computer, listening to music, and playing video games because they do them at the same time!

Social networking and the Internet have forever changed the way friends communicate. The days are gone when the only way to connect with friends was to see them face-to-face at school or talk for hours on the phone. Cell phones, the Internet, and social networking have made the world a smaller place. But that doesn't necessarily mean it's safer or better. No matter what the mode of media, there are specific guidelines about using it to keep in mind.

WORDS CAN HURT

When texting, remember that the people receiving your messages see only your words. They can't see your expressions or hear your tone of voice. They might think you are slamming them with words you meant as a joke. It's impossible to take back your words once you've pushed the button, so think before you send. How will the person on the receiving end react to your words? What will happen if others see what you wrote?

The same is true for any pictures or videos you might want to e-mail, post, tweet, or text. Good old Granny can help you there. Before you write those colorful words or snap that not-so-nice picture, ask yourself, "What would my grandmother say if she saw this?" If Grandma wouldn't approve, it's probably not a safe or appropriate thing to send.

NOTHING PERSONAL

Teens also need to be careful about making any personal information public. Never release personal information—such as your address, phone number, student ID, or Social Security number—via cell phone, e-mail, instant messages, or online networks. Don't post information online about your family either. Identity thieves look for such information to help them steal money by posing as you or a family member. Also, never agree

SAFETY ON SOCIAL NETWORKING SITES

Here are some tips for staying safe on social networking sites.
Don'ts:

- Don't share information told to you in confidence.
- Don't share information about your family.
- Don't reveal your full name, financial information, birthday, address, or phone number.
- Don't post pictures of your home or school.
- Don't post your location or specific plans with friends.

Dos:

- Do be suspicious and trust your instincts.
- Do check with and tell your friends and family if anyone contacts you that you don't know.
- Do think hard about posting a picture of yourself. It could be used to target you for harm.
- Do block people or choose not to respond if someone makes you uncomfortable.
- Do choose an online name that doesn't sound sexy or give away your real name.

to get together with someone that you meet online. It's too easy for people to pretend to be someone they're not: that sixteen-year-old guy that sounds really cute online could be old enough to be your grandfather.

Sexting, cyberbullying, and cheating are problems today's technology makes possible. Laws regulate some of these activities, and taking part could get you in trouble, hurting your chances for a great

Shared computer use can be fun. It's a good idea to show parents what you are doing regularly.

job or school in the future. College counselors and employers check Web sites and blogs, so make sure that what you put online doesn't put your reputation and future at risk.

FOLLOW THE RULES

Abide by age limits and follow the rules. You may be curious and want to visit some sites, but age limits and rules protect you from the frightening, upsetting, or confusing content they may contain. Age limits also guard you from coming in contact with online predators. Be sure to manage your privacy settings on social networking sites to protect against outsiders.

It's great to be independent, but being open with your parents or caretakers about your phone and computer use is a good safeguard. If you keep them in your online loop, they can help you spot trouble and be there in case you need help.

10 GREAT QUESTIONS
TO ASK A COUNSELOR

 WHAT SHOULD I LOOK FOR IN A FRIEND?

 MY FRIENDS ARE USING DRUGS/ALCOHOL. WHAT SHOULD I DO?

 HOW DO I KNOW WHEN TO TELL OR KEEP A FRIEND'S SECRET?

 IS THERE SUCH A THING AS BEING TOO SHY TO MAKE FRIENDS?

 WHY DOESN'T ANYONE LIKE ME?

 I'M JEALOUS BECAUSE MY BEST FRIEND HAS A BOYFRIEND OR GIRLFRIEND. WHAT CAN I DO?

 WHAT CAN I DO ABOUT A FRIEND WHO IS BULLYING SOMEONE ONLINE?

 HOW DO I TELL A FRIEND TO STOP TEXTING ME ALL THE TIME WITHOUT HURTING MY FRIEND'S FEELINGS?

 HOW CAN I TELL MY FRIEND HE OR SHE IS BEING TOO CLINGY?

 TWO OF MY FRIENDS ARE VERY CLOSE WITH EACH OTHER, AND I OFTEN FEEL LEFT OUT. WHAT SHOULD I DO?

WEATHER THE BUMPS

As much as we'd like to think all our friendships will last forever, many don't. People, situations, and interests change. Families move, and seniors graduate. Like leaves on the water, we drift apart. But knowing this happens to everybody can make it easier to take. Change is just one of the bumps we must weather when we open ourselves to making friends.

Like teeter-totters, there are ups and downs in relationships. Only once in a while do things balance out. One way to keep things in balance more often is to learn how to negotiate. Sounds like something only company CEOs do, right? Wrong! You've been negotiating since you first talked a parent into letting you stay up past your bedtime. According to the Merriam-Webster online dictionary, to negotiate is "to confer with another so as to arrive at a settlement of some matter." Let's say you are dying to go to the Halloween Chillibration,

HOW TO HELP WHEN FRIENDS ARE BLUE

If your friend is having a hard time, you may want to help but not know how. Here are some ideas for helping a friend through bad times:

- Reach out and let your friend know you care.
- Really listen. Nod and make remarks to show you are paying attention: "I hear you." "That's the pits."
- Resist offering solutions.
- Invite the friend to join you in an activity you know he or she enjoys.
- Avoid spouting clichés such as, "Cheer up," "Keep your chin up," or "These things happen for a reason."

When a friend is hurting, sometimes your caring gesture can be just what he or she needs.

but your friend wants to go shopping. You can negotiate with your friend to spend two hours shopping and then attend the Chillibration later.

LEARN TO COMPROMISE

Learning to compromise is a part of negotiating, too. Friends compromise by agreeing to meet in the middle. So instead of the Halloween party or shopping, you may take in a movie you both want to see and save the other activities for when you aren't together.

The teeter-totter sometimes gets off balance if one person doesn't give the other person enough space. When a friend has low self-esteem, the person's fear of not being included can

WHEN A FRIENDSHIP ENDS

Friendships end, but although it is painful, you will survive. Here are some things to remember when a friend says good-bye:

- It's OK to grieve. The end of a friendship is a loss, similar to a death. It's normal to be sad about it.
- Let go gracefully. Clinging and trying to hold on to the friend will only make you both miserable.
- Forgive yourself if you did something to cause the breakup of the friendship.
- Remember the good times you had together.
- If you are ending the friendship, be honest and let the person know why.
- Think about what you learned from the relationship.
- Move on, and make new friends.

49

make him or her act like a leech—latching on and always wanting to be together. But this leechlike behavior can suck the fun out of a friendship, leaving the leech even more needy and the leeched angry. If it feels like a friend is getting clingy, voice your concerns. Kindly tell the friend that although you like the company, you need some space at times, too. Set a time for when you'll get together again, but let the friend know you'll be busy in the meantime. Use your parents as an excuse if necessary (be sure to clear it with them first).

If you're the leech, remember to be respectful of your friend's wishes. Everyone needs space, and it's no reflection on how close your friendship is. Find others to hang out with in the meantime and enjoy your time apart.

When a problem arises in a friendship, talking about it is the best option.

SLIPUPS HAPPEN

No matter how close, friends are bound to hurt each other at some time. Your friend let it slip that you like the new guy in biology, and you could just scream. She's apologized, but you're still mad. You could tell everybody one of her secrets to get back at her. But getting revenge just keeps the fight going, which is not fun for either of you. Chances are, the best thing to do is the hardest—forgive. We all mess up. Think about how you would like your friend to react when you do it the next time.

Having a good sense of humor helps, too. Often tempers flare when people are stressed, and friends say things they wouldn't normally say. At those times, a laugh may be all it takes to set things right between friends.

Not everything can be solved easily, however. What if your friend is having personal or family problems? What if he or she is involved in risky behavior? At these times you may not know how to react, and the best thing you can do is find outside help.

French poet Jacques Delille once said, "Fate chooses our relatives, but we choose our friends." Friends are gifts we get to pick out for ourselves. Learning how to choose them and treat them well are skills we will treasure for a lifetime.

GLOSSARY

CLIQUE A small group of select friends.

COMPROMISE An agreement of differences in which both sides give up part of their demands.

CONFIDENCE Belief in oneself.

CYBERBULLYING Use of the Internet and digital technologies to torment, harass, or target a person.

FRIEND A person who is attached to another by affection or esteem.

NEGOTIATE To bargain for an agreement.

PARALANGUAGE Nonverbal elements in speech, such as tone and volume of voice, that help communicate meaning.

PEER A person of the same social group or age.

PEER PRESSURE Social pressure by members of a person's peer group to act a certain way, adopt certain values, or go along with the group's wishes.

PREDATOR A person who victimizes another person for his or her own gain and for illegal purposes.

SELF-ESTEEM Respect for oneself.

SEXTING Sending photos or messages with sexual content by a mobile device, such as a cell phone.

SEXUAL ORIENTATION People's natural preference for which gender(s) they are sexually attracted to.

SHYNESS Discomfort and lack of confidence in social situations; bashfulness; timidity.

SIBLING A brother or a sister.

SOCIAL NETWORKING Communicating via connected profiles on social Web sites.

Boys & Girls Clubs of America
1275 Peachtree Street NE
Atlanta, GA 30309-3506
(404) 487-5700
Web site: http://www.bgca.org
Boys & Girls Clubs are located all over the United
States and offer after-school and summer programs
to provide young people with safe places to learn,
grow, and make new friends.

Boys & Girls Clubs of Canada
7100 Woodbine Avenue, Suite 204
Markham, ON L3R 5J2
Canada
(905) 477-7272
Web site: http://www.bgccan.com
The mission of the Boys & Girls Clubs of Canada is to
provide a safe, supportive place where children and
youth can experience new opportunities, build positive relationships, and develop confidence and skills
for life.

Boy Scouts of America (BSA)
1325 W. Walnut Hill Lane
Irving, TX 75015-2079
(972) 580-2219
Web site: http://www.scouting.org
Boy Scouts of America is one of the largest organiza-
tions for youth development. The BSA provides a

program that develops character, citizenship skills, and personal fitness. The organization provides learning experiences and friendship-building activities for boys of all ages.

4-H
National Headquarters
1400 Independence Avenue SW, Stop 2225
Washington, DC 20250-2225
(202) 401-4114
Web site: http://www.4-h.org
The 4-H youth organization is a community of more than 6.5 million young people across America. Participants engage in hands-on learning activities in the areas of science, citizenship, and healthy living. 4-H provides leadership opportunities for youth in both rural and urban communities.

Girl Scouts of the USA
420 Fifth Avenue
New York, NY 10018-2798
(800) 478-7248
Web site: http://www.girlscouts.org
Girl Scouts provides girls of all ages the opportunity to learn and grow and to experience the fun, friendship, and power of girls together. The organization's mission is to build girls of courage, confidence, and character, who make the world a better place.

Scouts Canada
1345 Baseline Road
Ottawa, ON K2C 0A7
Canada
(888) 726-8876
Web site: http://www.scouts.ca
Scouts Canada supports young people ages five through twenty-six, providing fun, friendship, and challenging programs to help them build confidence and be successful. Programs bring a world of adventure and outdoor experience to Canadian youth.

YMCA of the USA
101 N. Wacker Drive
Chicago, IL 60606
(800) 872-9622
Web site: http://www.ymca.net
The YMCA provides community-based programs that bring people of all ages and backgrounds together to foster healthy lifestyles and nurture the potential of youth.

WEB SITES

Due to the changing nature of Internet links, Rosen Publishing has developed an online list of Web sites related to the subject of this book. This site is updated regularly. Please use this link to access the list:

http://www.rosenlinks.com/top10/frnd

Bailey, Diane. *Girls: Being Best Friends* (Relationships 101). New York, NY: Rosen Publishing, 2012.

Basen, Ryan. *Got Your Back: Dealing with Friends and Enemies* (A Guy's Guide). Edina, MN: ABDO Publishing, 2011.

Burns, Jan. *Friendship: A How-To Guide* (Life: A How-To Guide). Berkeley Heights, NJ: Enslow Publishers, Inc., 2011.

Cook, Colleen Ryckert. *Frequently Asked Questions About Social Networking* (FAQ: Teen Life). New York, NY: Rosen Publishing, 2011.

Diamond, Susan, and Ann Gordon. *Social Rules for Kids: The Top 100 Social Rules Kids Need to Succeed*. Shawnee Mission, KS: AAPC Publishing, 2011.

Doeden, Matt. *Conflict Resolution Smarts: How to Communicate, Negotiate, Compromise, and More* (USA Today Teen Wise Guides: Time, Money, and Relationships). Minneapolis, MN: Twenty-First Century Books, 2012.

Dowell, Frances O'Roark. *The Kind of Friends We Used to Be*. New York, NY: Atheneum Books for Young Readers, 2009.

Erskine, Kathryn. *Mockingbird*. New York, NY: Philomel Books, 2010.

Flynn, Sarah Wassner. *Girls' Life Guide to a Drama-Free Life*. New York, NY: Scholastic, 2010.

Heos, Bridget. *Guys: Being Best Friends* (Relationships 101). New York, NY: Rosen Publishing, 2012.

Jones, Carrie, and Megan Kelley Hall. *Dear Bully: 70 Authors Tell Their Stories*. New York, NY: HarperTeen, 2011.

Kitanidis, Phoebe. *Fab Girls Guide to Friendship Hardship* (Discovery Girls). San Jose, CA: Discovery Girls, Inc., 2007.

Levin, Judith. *Frequently Asked Questions About When a Friendship Ends* (FAQ: Teen Life). New York, NY: Rosen Publishing, 2008.

Markovics, Joyce L. *Relationship Smarts: How to Navigate Dating, Friendships, Family Relationships, and More* (USA Today Teen Wise Guides: Time, Money, and Relationships). Minneapolis, MN: Twenty-First Century Books, 2012.

Meyer, Jared. *Making Friends: The Art of Social Networking in Life and Online* (Communicating with Confidence). New York, NY: Rosen Publishing, 2012.

Schmidt, Gary D. *Okay for Now*. New York, NY: Clarion Books, 2011.

BIBLIOGRAPHY

Adoption.com. "The Joys and Complexities of Sibling Relationships." Retrieved September 2011 (http://library.adoption.com/articles/the-joys-and-complexities-of-sibling-relationships.html).

Barker, Joanne. "Teens and Peer Pressure." WebMD, 2011. Retrieved September 2011 (http://www.webmd.com/parenting/teen-abuse-cough-medicine-9/peer-pressure).

Blume, L. B., and M. J. Zembar. "Peer Relations in Middle Childhood." Excerpted from *Middle Childhood to Middle Adolescence: Development from Ages 8 to 18*. Upper Saddle River, NJ: Prentice Hall, 2007. Education.com. Retrieved September 2011 (http://www.education.com/reference/article/peer-relations-middle-childhood).

Bonior, Andrea. *The Friendship Fix: The Complete Guide to Choosing, Losing, and Keeping Up with Your Friends*. New York, NY: Thomas Dunne Books, 2011.

Centers for Disease Control and Prevention. "Teaching Your Teen." March 5, 2010. Retrieved September 2011 (http://www.cdc.gov/chooserespect/at_home/teaching_your_teen.html).

Duke, Marshall P., Stephen Nowicki, and Elisabeth A. Martin. *Teaching Your Child the Language of Social Success*. Atlanta, GA: Peachtree Publishers, 1996.

Elman, Natalie Madorsky, and Eileen Kennedy-Moore. *The Unwritten Rules of Friendship: Simple Strategies to Help Your Child Make Friends*. Boston, MA: Little, Brown, 2003.

Freeman, Shanna. "How to Be Happy in a Relationship: Learning to Listen." TLC Family. Retrieved September 2011 (http://health.howstuffworks.com/ mental-health/human-nature/happiness/happy-in-a -relationship4.htm/printable).

Golden, Tom. "Gender Differences in Boys' and Girls' Emotions." Education.com. Retrieved September 2011 (http://www.education.com/print/ Ref_Boys_Girls_Emotions).

Goodman, Robin F. NYU Child Study Center. "Friends and Friendships." Education.com. Retrieved September 2011 (http://www.education.com/ reference/article/Ref_Friends_Friendships_1).

Grohol, John M. "Become a Better Listener: Active Listening." PsychCentral.com, 2007. Retrieved October 2011 (http://psychcentral.com/lib/2007/ become-a-better-listener-active-listening).

Healy, Vikki Ortiz. "Power Packs: Teens Today Prefer Friendship in Groups." *Chicago Tribune*, September 26, 2010. Retrieved September 2011 (http:// articles.chicagotribune.com/2010-09-26/news/ ct-met-teen-friendship-0926-20100926_1 _teen-cliques-friend-power-packs).

Herron, Ron, and Val J. Peter. *A Good Friend: How to Make One, How to Be One* (Boys Town Teens and Relationships). Boys Town, NE: Boys Town Press, 1998.

Josephson Institute of Ethics. "The Six Pillars of Character: Trustworthiness, Respect, Responsibility,

Fairness, Caring, Citizenship." 2011. Retrieved September 2011 (http://josephsoninstitute.org/sixpillars.html).

Kraut, Richard. "Aristotle's Ethics." Stanford Encyclopedia of Philosophy, March 29, 2010. Retrieved August 2011 (http://plato.stanford.edu/entries/aristotle-ethics).

Lutz, Ericka. *The Complete Idiot's Guide to Friendship for Teens*. Indianapolis, IN: Alpha Books, 2001.

Nauert, Rick. "Middle-School Friends Are Critical for Future Success." PsychCentral.com, January 13, 2011. Retrieved September 2011 (http://psychcentral.com/news/2011/01/13/middle-school-friends-are-critical-for-future-success/22593.html).

Nemours Foundation. "How Can I Improve My Self-Esteem?" TeensHealth.org, March 2009. Retrieved August 2011 (http://teenshealth.org/teen/your_mind/mental_health/self_esteem.html#cat20123).

Nemours Foundation. "Peer Pressure." TeensHealth.org, March 2009. Retrieved August 2011 (http://kidshealth.org/teen/your_mind/friends/peer_pressure.html).

Nielsen Company. "Kids Today: How the Class of 2011 Engages with Media." June 8, 2011. Retrieved September 2011 (http://blog.nielsen.com/nielsen-wire/consumer/kids-today-how-the-class-of-2011-engages-with-media).

Parker-Pope, Tara. "What Are Friends For? A Longer Life." *New York Times*, April 20, 2009. Retrieved August 2011 (http://www.nytimes.com/2009/04/21/health/21well.html).

Perkins, Daniel F., and Kate Fogarty. "Active Listening: A Communication Tool." University of Florida IFAS Extension, Document FCS2151, June 2005. Retrieved September 2011 (http://edis.ifas.ufl.edu/pdffiles/HE/HE36100.pdf).

Torppa, Cynthia Burggraf. "Gender Issues: Communication Differences in Interpersonal Relationships." Ohio State University, 2010. Retrieved September 2011 (http://ohioline.osu.edu/flm02/pdf/fs04.pdf).

Torppa, Cynthia Burggraf. "Nonverbal Communication: Teaching Your Child the Skills of Social Success." Ohio State University, 2009. Retrieved September 2011 (http://ohioline.osu.edu/flm03/FS10.pdf).

Walker, Joyce. "Teens in Distress: Helping Friends in Trouble: Stress, Depression, and Suicide." University of Minnesota Extension, 2005. Retrieved September 2011 (http://www.extension.umn.edu/distribution/youthdevelopment/da2787.html).

INDEX

A

acquaintances, 8
advice, giving, 27
age limits, 45
alcohol, 37, 46
anger, 12, 17, 28, 31

B

best friends, 4, 24, 29, 40, 48
BFFs, 4
body bubbles, 17
body language, 16, 20, 28, 31
bullying, 37, 44, 46
breakups, 49

C

cliques, 11, 41
communication, unwritten rules of,
    16–20
compliments, 18, 24, 32
compromise, learning to,
    49–50
conflicts, avoiding, 25
conversation basics, 30–33
counselor, 10 great questions to
    ask a, 46
cyberbullying, 44

D

depression, 6, 29
drugs, 37, 46

E

exit strategies, 35
eye contact, making, 17, 18,
    27, 31

F

friendship
    benefits of, 6, 29
    changes in a, 11, 47–51
    families and, 11, 33, 36, 40
    good characteristics, 9, 23
    myths and facts, 29
    overview, 4–11, 16
    unhealthy signs, 10, 37
    with yourself, 6, 12–15

G

gay friends, 38–39
give and take, learning to, 34–37
goals, setting, 15
gossiping, 33
group friendships, 40–41

H

honesty, need for, 21–22, 23,
    39, 49
humor, using, 39, 43, 51

I

identity theft, 43
"I" messages, 32–33

instant messaging, 43
instincts, trusting your, 35, 44

J

jealousy, 46

L

listening skills, 9, 20, 25–28,
    31, 48

M

"Me" lists, 14–15, 34
mixed messages, 20

N

negative thinking, 14, 18, 39
negotiating, 47, 49
no, saying, 22–23, 35, 37
nonverbal cues, 17

O

online safety, 42–45
opposite-sex friendships, 29,
    38–39

P

paralanguage, 16, 18

peer pressure, 35, 37
privacy settings, 45

R

rumors, spreading, 33

S

sarcasm, 31
secrets, keeping, 23, 33, 46
self-esteem, improving, 13–14,
    39, 41
sexting, 44
sexual orientation, 39
shoplifting, 37
shyness, 12, 13, 18, 46
Sibling Bond, The, 40
smoking, 35, 37
social networking, 42, 43, 44, 45

T

teasing, 29, 37, 39
texting, 5, 23, 27, 30, 42,
    43, 46
true self, being your,
    21–24, 39
trust, developing, 23

Y

"you" messages, 32–33

ABOUT THE AUTHOR

Dale-Marie Bryan is the author of six books for young people. She has been making friends for over fifty years and enjoys meeting new friends when she presents work-shops as a curriculum writer and educator.

PHOTO CREDITS

Cover © iStockphoto.com/Grady Reese; p. 5 Steve Mason/Photodisc/Thinkstock; p. 8 BananaStock/Thinkstock; pp. 9, 48 Ingram Publishing/Thinkstock; p. 14 Ryan McVay/Photodisc/Thinkstock; p. 17 Comstock/Thinkstock; p. 19 Stockbyte/Thinkstock; p. 22 shy/Shutterstock.com; pp. 26, 50 iStockphoto/Thinkstock; p. 31 Yellow Dog Productions/The Image Bank/Getty Images; p. 36 David Young-Wolff/Stone/Getty Images; p. 40 Petrenko Andriy/Shutterstock.com; p. 45 Todd Warnock/Lifesize/Thinkstock; cover and interior background graphics phyZick/Shutterstock.com.

Designer: Nicole Russo; Editor: Andrea Sclarow Paskoff; Photo Researcher: Karen Huang